LITTLE BEAR MARCHES IN THE ST. PATRICK'S DAY PARADE

by Janice and illustrated by Mariana

Lothrop, Lee & Shepard Co.

NEW YORK

"My, I'm hungry," said Little Bear, as he opened his eyes. Then he yawned a great big yawn. It was the month of March, and Little Bear was just waking up from his winter sleep.

He climbed out of bed and went to the cupboard. He took down a box of cornflakes and a can of milk. He poured *all* the cornflakes and *all* the milk into a blue bowl, tied a napkin around his neck and went back to bed to eat his breakfast.

Just then a tiny voice said, "Little Bear, Little Bear, are you awake yet?" It was Squeaky, the Mouse.

"Yes," roared Little Bear. Little Bear climbed out of bed and opened the door. Squeaky was standing on the doorstep wet with rain and dragging a closed umbrella behind him.

"What's that?" asked Little Bear.

"It's an umbrella I found. If you want to go out when it rains, you open it up and then the rain can't touch you. You take it, Little Bear. It's too big for me."

"Thank you, Squeaky," said Little Bear. "Let's go out right away." But then he remembered his cornflakes. "I mean as soon as we've had breakfast."

Squeaky's eyes shone. "I *am* rather hungry," he said.

Little Bear put a spoonful of cornflakes and a teaspoon of milk into a saucer for Squeaky.

Then they both climbed into Little Bear's
bed and ate their breakfast. When there
wasn't a single cornflake left, Little Bear
said, "Now lick your plate and I'll lick
mine. Then we won't have to wash them."

So they licked their plates until they
shone. "Now," said Little Bear, "let's go
out for a walk."

"Don't forget the umbrella," said
Squeaky.

Outside it was raining very hard. All the trees were dripping and the ground was squishy-squashy. Little Bear opened the umbrella and he and Squeaky started out toward the village.

"Isn't it wonderful to have an umbrella?" said Little Bear. But they hadn't walked more than a few minutes when it stopped raining.

"Oh," said Little Bear, "it's not raining any more. I'll take the umbrella home."

So they walked back to Little Bear's house, left the umbrella to dry in the bathtub, and started to walk to the village again.

Before they turned the corner PLOP PLOP
PLOP it began to rain again.

"Let's go back and get the umbrella,"
said Little Bear. So they ran back to the
house, picked up the umbrella and started
off for the village again.

Squirrel saw them coming. "What a fine umbrella you have, Little Bear. But can't you see it has stopped raining?"

"It *has?*" said Little Bear. He scratched his head. "Do you think I should take the umbrella back?"

Squeaky looked at the sky for a long time.

"Yes," he said at last. "I think it has stopped raining for keeps."

So they ran back to Little Bear's house for the third time, put the umbrella in the hall closet and started to walk back to the village.

By the time they got to the garden gate PLOP PLOP PLOP it began to rain again.

"It's raining *again!* Let's get the umbrella," said Little Bear. So they ran back once more and got the umbrella out of the closet. The minute Little Bear opened it, the rain stopped.

"There's something very strange about that umbrella," said Squeaky. "Let me think." He sat down on the doorstep, put his head in his hands, curled his tail around his middle, and thought.

"You know what, Little Bear?" he said
at last. "I think it is a magic umbrella."
"It is?" asked Little Bear.
"It really is," said Squeaky.
By this time the sun was shining.

"Let's make it rain again," said Little
Bear. He closed the umbrella, and PLOP
PLOP PLOP it began to rain again.

"Now, let's make it stop." He opened the
umbrella and immediately the sun came
out. They did this all day until Little Bear
got tired of opening and closing the umbrella.

The next day Little Bear and Squeaky
felt lazy, so they stayed home.

Outside it rained. Everyone stayed home.
No one went to the store to buy anything.
Even the children didn't go out to play.

And Mr. Summer, the Mayor, was very worried. "If it rains like this," he said, "we won't be able to have the St. Patrick's Day Parade."

Not have the St. Patrick's Day Parade? The children couldn't think of anything worse.

That night after supper Little Bear said, "I'm tired. I'm going to bed and sleep until next month."

On St. Patrick's Day the weather was
TERRIBLE. First it snowed, then it hailed,
then it rained.

"Oh dear, oh dear," said the Mayor. "We
can't possibly have the parade in this
weather."

"But we must have it," said the school-
master. "Everybody is ready. Everybody is
dressed in green and the band has been
practicing all winter."

"I know someone who can stop the rain," said Squeaky. "It's Little Bear."

"Nonsense," said the Mayor. "How can Little Bear stop the rain?"

"Wait and see," said Squeaky, and he ran to Little Bear's house.

He knocked. No answer. He knocked again. No answer.

"Little Bear," he called out in a loud voice. "Are you there?"

"Huh?" said Little Bear in his sleep.

"Wake up, Little Bear. The Mayor needs you."

So Little Bear woke up and let Squeaky in.

"Little Bear, the Mayor is in terrible trouble. If you don't come with your magic umbrella, he won't be able to have the St. Patrick's Day Parade this year."

"I'll come," said Little Bear. They hurried over to the Mayor's house and Little Bear agreed to stop the rain. "But I would like to have a green hat and march in the parade," Little Bear said.

"Of course! Of course!" said the Mayor. "Anything you like."

So Little Bear took his umbrella and went with the Mayor to the village square. As soon as he opened the umbrella, it stopped raining.

"Now the parade can begin," said the Mayor. "It has stopped raining just in time."

"It was Little Bear who did it," said Squeaky. "And you promised he could march in the parade and wear a green hat."

"Oh, now! We can't have a little bear in a St. Patrick's Day Parade," said the Mayor.

"But you promised," Squeaky said.

"But that's ridiculous. Parades are for children. And I'm sure it wasn't Little Bear who stopped the rain."

As soon as Little Bear heard this, he closed his umbrella and went home. *It began to rain harder than ever.* The parade couldn't begin.

"Now do you believe me?" asked Squeaky.

The Mayor hesitated.

"WE WANT LITTLE BEAR! WE WANT LITTLE BEAR!" the children shouted.

"All right," said the Mayor. "Tell Little Bear I'm sorry and he *can* march in the parade."

So Squeaky went to Little Bear's house and said, "Little Bear, please come back and stop the rain."

But Little Bear wouldn't.

"Little Bear, you can have a green hat and march in the parade. The Mayor said so."

But Little Bear wouldn't.

"Little Bear, you can have the green hat, march in the parade and BEAT THE DRUM!"

"*Yes! Yes!*" cried Little Bear. He ran with Squeaky all the way to the village square.

And Little Bear marched proudly at the head of the parade.

He wore a green hat. He beat the drum
with his right paw and carried the umbrella
with his left.

And Squeaky stood on his shoulder
shouting, "Hip-Hip-Hurray!"